Elliot Minds the Store

By Marcy Kelman
Illustrated by Alan Batson
Based on the episode written by Lorne Cameron

DISNEP PRESS

NEW YORK

Copyright © 2009 by Disney Enterprises, Inc. All rights reserved. Published by Disney Press,
an imprint of Disney Book Group. No part of this book may be reproduced or transmitted
in any form or by any means, electronic or mechanical, including photocopying, recording, or
by any information storage and retrieval system, without written permission from the publisher.
For information address Disney Press, 114 Fifth Avenue, New York, New York 10011-5690.

First Edition 10 9 8 7 6 5 4 3 2 1
Library of Congress Cataloging-in-Publication Data on file
ISBN 978-1-4231-1757-5

Manufactured in the USA
For more Disney Press fun, visit www.disneybooks.com

Manny and the tools had a busy week ahead of them.

"Putting the work schedule up here will definitely help the shop run more smoothly," Manny said as he tacked the schedule to the bulletin board. "Thanks for the great idea, Stretch."

Stretch blushed. "Aw, well, it's really no big deal."

"You can say that again," grumbled Turner. "Hmmph! Anyone could have come up with that idea!"

"*You* didn't!" Felipe reminded Turner.

"Yeah, well…that's because I was too busy coming up with an even *better* way to organize the workshop!" Turner said with a sneer.

Felipe rolled his eyes. "Well, come on, Turner. The world is waiting to hear this most *inteligente* idea from the sharpest tool in the toolbox!"

"That's funny." Pat smiled. "People are always telling me that I'm not the sharpest tool in the toolbox, which makes sense since I don't have any sharp points!"

"You can say that again," Felipe muttered.

"Gee, I think I win for sharpest points," Dusty said with a laugh. "But, okay, go ahead with your big idea, Turner."

Turner started to cough and clear his throat. "Ahem, let's see...okay...er...ooh, I know! Let's take all the paperwork, put it on a clipboard, and then hang the clipboard on the bulletin board!"

Felipe yawned. "Ho-hum, speaking of 'bored'..."

"Well, it can't hurt to try!" suggested Manny. He tacked the clipboard to the bulletin board.

But within a few seconds, the whole bulletin board came crashing to the floor!

Stretch peered out from under a sheet of paper. "I hope you don't mind me correcting you, Manny, but, yes… sometimes it *can* hurt to try!"

"Sorry about that, Stretch," said Manny. "Wait a minute—where's Felipe?"

With a big groan, Felipe pried himself out from under the bulletin board. "Here's a bulletin: I think we need to add 'Clean up Turner's Bad Idea' to Stretch's work schedule!"

Rusty surveyed the mess and started to worry. "Now what are we going to do?!"

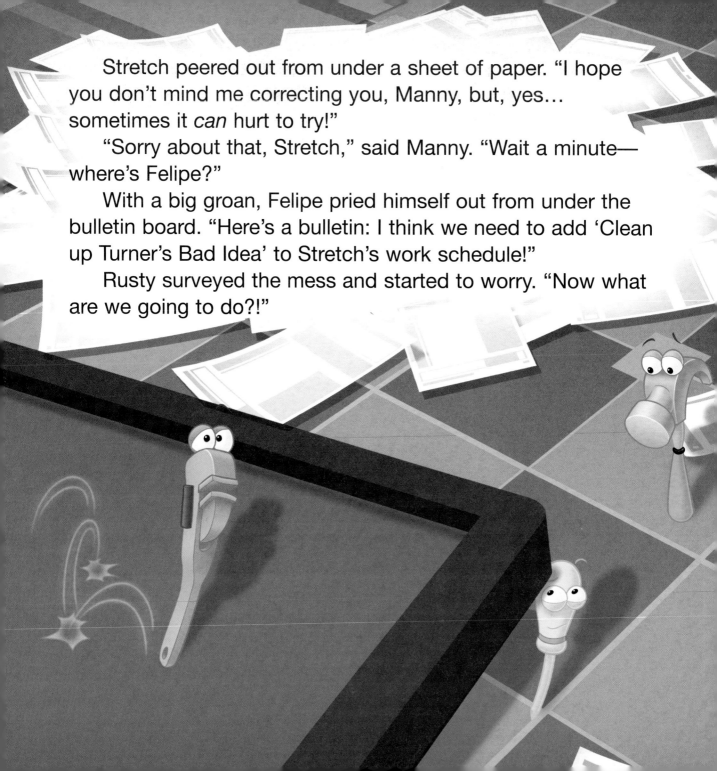

"Well, the first thing we need to do is to buy a stronger hook—especially if you guys plan on coming up with more great ideas." Manny chuckled. "Good thing that we were headed to Kelly's this morning anyway."

"We were?" asked Turner.

"Ah, yes, let me inform those who weren't lucky enough to have the work schedule—oh, and an entire bulletin board—land on their faces," Felipe wisecracked. "We're scheduled to help Kelly set up for her super sale this morning!"

On their way to Kelly's Hardware Store, Manny and the tools saw Mr. Lopart jogging along the sidewalk.

"*Buenos días*, Mr. Lopart," greeted Manny.

Mr. Lopart was out of breath. "Hoo! Good…day…to… you… too… Manny," he said, stretching from side to side.

"What are you doing, Mr. Lopart?" asked Squeeze.

"Warming up!" explained Mr. Lopart. "I want to make sure I'm the first one through the door at Kelly's super sale today. That way I can get the best bargains!"

"Hey, that's where we're going—to Kelly's Hardware Store," said Dusty.

Mr. Lopart was alarmed. "WHAT? You're going there now? B-b-b-but the sale doesn't start until ten o'clock!"

"Don't worry," Manny assured him. "We're just getting there early to help Kelly set up for the super *venta*—the sale!"

"Super!" exclaimed Mr. Lopart. "See you at the *venta*!"

"I'll be with you in a second, guys," Kelly said when Manny and the tools entered her hardware store. "All right, let's go over it one more time, Elliot. If someone asks for a part, and you don't know where it is, what do you do?"

"Um, just a second…it's coming to me…" Elliot thought hard as he tapped two pencils against the counter like drumsticks.

"You look it up in the parts catalog, right?" Kelly reminded him.

"Yeah, totally!" said Elliot. "That's all I need to know, right?"

"No, Elliot, then you've got to find the part and ring it up on the cash register, remember?" said Kelly.

Elliot started to blush. "Oh, yeah, I always forget that part."

Kelly turned to Manny and the tools. "Elliot's going to help me with the sale today."

"That's great!" Squeeze beamed. "We're helping out too, right?"

"Yes! I need you guys to fasten my brand-new display to the wall," Kelly explained. "It would be a big disaster if it fell."

"Don't worry, Kelly. We have a lot of expertise when it comes to disasters and things falling," Felipe joked. "Right, Turner?"

"Argh, that *joke* was a disaster," Turner said with a snort.

"Speaking of disasters, we need to buy a strong hook for our bulletin board," Rusty said.

"No problem!" said Kelly. "I was just going to grab a quick breakfast before the sale starts, but I'm sure Elliot could help you with that."

"Me? Oh, I d-d-don't know," Elliot sputtered. "I mean, if this were a skateboard store or a drum shop, I might be able to help them out. But hardware supplies?"

"You'll do fine, Elliot," Kelly promised as she headed for the front door. "Besides, with Manny as your first customer, how hard could it be? I'll be back before you know it. Bye, guys!"

Elliot stood for awhile and just looked at Manny nervously. "Um, m-m-may I help you?" he said finally.

"Yes. The bulletin board at my workshop fell down today, so we need a stronger hook to hold it up," Manny explained. Elliot froze, unsure what to do. "Uh, maybe you should look it up in the parts catalog?" Manny suggested.

"Right, of course!" Elliot grabbed a catalog from the counter and searched through it. "Hook, hook…Oh, here it is: 'Hook, Charles…1130 Leeside Lane'!"

"I think that might be the phone book, Elliot," Manny offered.

"Heh, I guess you could say that the hardware business just isn't his *calling*!" Turner whispered to Felipe.

Elliot finally found the parts catalog, but it wasn't long before he dropped the heavy book on his foot!

"Here, let me help you with that," Manny said, picking up the catalog and finding the page Elliot needed. After reading the part's description, Elliot ran to the stockroom to find the right hook.

"Found it!" Elliot declared, proudly handing the hook to Manny.

"Yep, that's it. Great job, Elliot," said Manny.

"Cool, dude—oops, I mean, Manny. Well, thanks for stopping by. See you soon!" Elliot said, waving good-bye to Manny.

"Um, aren't you going to ring up our purchase on the cash register?" asked Felipe.

Elliot was disappointed. "Bummer! I knew I forgot something. I'm so totally bad at this!"

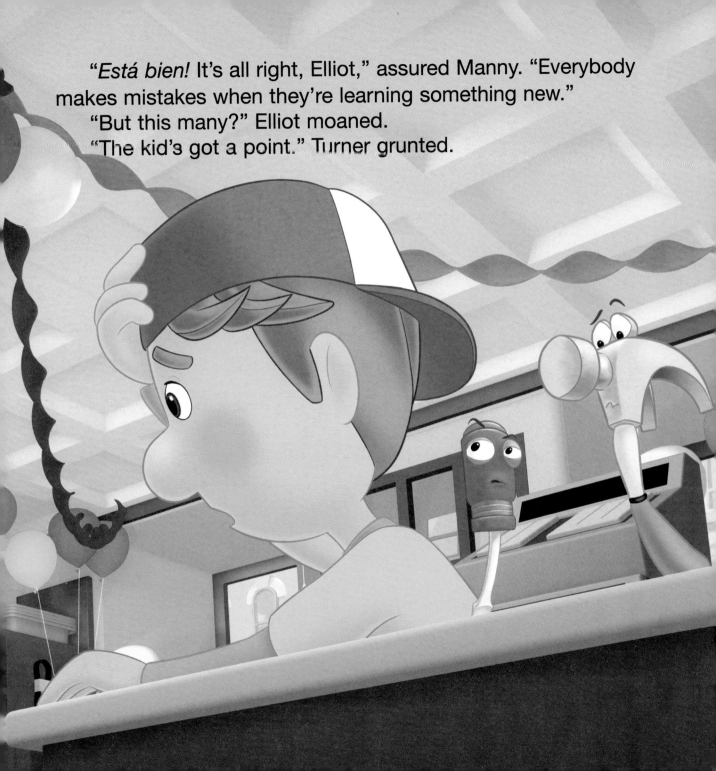

"*Está bien!* It's all right, Elliot," assured Manny. "Everybody makes mistakes when they're learning something new."

"But this many?" Elliot moaned.

"The kid's got a point." Turner grunted.

"Well, the important thing is to learn from your mistakes…so you can be ready the next time," said Manny.

Elliot began ringing up Manny's purchase at the cash register. "That'll be five hundred dollars, please!"

Manny couldn't believe his ears. "For a hook? Are you sure?"

"Oops, my bad! I read it wrong. It's actually just five dollars."

As Elliot fumbled with the keys for the cash register, his sleeve got caught in the register's drawer. "Aw, man, now I'm stuck!"

Squeeze jumped into action and helped yank Elliot's sleeve out of the register drawer. Elliot looked frazzled.

Manny was concerned. "Elliot, are you all right?"

"Aw, it's no use. I can't do this! If it's not a skateboard or a drum set, I'm completely useless," Elliot said with a sigh.

"Don't be so hard on yourself, Elliot," Dusty said.

"You just need a little confidence," added Turner.

"Turner's right," agreed Manny. "You just have to believe in yourself."

"Well, how can I do that?" wondered Elliot.

"It's easy," reasoned Felipe. "If you look confident, you'll feel confident. And if you feel *seguro*, you'll be *seguro*."

But at that moment, Elliot just couldn't look or feel very confident at all. "I can't believe one dude can mess up so much," he said, shaking his head.

Stretch had an idea. "You know, I always heard that if you do something that you're good at, confidence is sure to follow. So why don't you go get your skateboard?"

Manny looked nervous. "Um, I don't think skateboarding in Kelly's shop is such a good idea, Stretch."

"Don't worry, I know what I'm doing." Stretch beamed.

Manny covered his eyes as Stretch encouraged Elliot to try out a few skateboarding moves inside the shop. Elliot zipped and zoomed around the aisles with ease.

"Now how do you feel?" Stretch asked Elliot.

"You were right!" Elliot exclaimed, flipping up his skateboard and catching it with one hand. "I feel awesome!"

As he jumped up and let out a big "YES," Elliot lost his footing and bumped right into Kelly's new display, sending it crashing down to the floor!

Elliot couldn't believe his eyes. He started to panic. "Oh, no! I made things even worse, and Kelly's going to be back any minute. What am I going to do?"

"Hang on a second, Elliot. I have an idea," said Manny. "You know, the balance you showed on your skateboard might just come in handy for piecing that display back together!"

"Really?" Elliot was shocked.

"Yes, and that drumming of yours is perfect for using a hammer, such as Pat," Manny explained.

"Are you saying that I could actually fix the shelf before Kelly gets back? ME?" Elliot asked in disbelief.

"Well, with a little help, I don't see why not," said Manny. "You just have to believe in yourself."

The fact that Manny believed Elliot was capable of fixing the display gave Elliot the confidence to try. Using a shelf like a skateboard, Elliot rounded up all of the spray paints that fell on the floor by "skating" them back to the display area.

Then, with Pat's help, Elliot put his drumming skills to work and hammered the shelves back into place.

Manny and the tools worked quickly to put all the hardware supplies back into Kelly's display…just as she had them originally.

When he stepped back to look at the final result, Manny congratulated Elliot on the great work he had done. "*Muy bien*, Elliot. Very good! See? You have more talents than you thought you did!"

"You're right. I should have believed in myself all along," said Elliot. "Thanks, Manny. Thanks, tools."

Just then, Kelly returned to the shop. "I'm back! Any problems while I was gone?"

"Nothing I couldn't handle," Elliot replied with a big grin. "Uh, with a little help from my friends, that is!"

Kelly was pleased. "Thank you, Elliot. You did a great job. Oh, it's almost ten o'clock! I'd better open the store for business."

As soon as Kelly opened the front door, Mr. Lopart came barreling in at top speed. "You see? I told you I'd be the first one through the door for the super *saaaaaaale*!" Mr. Lopart tripped over Manny's toolbox and landed on the floor!

"Well, that was a super *sail*—you sailed right into my toolbox!" joked Manny.

Elliot laughed. "Guess it's not just the prices that are falling today, huh?"